DISNEY · PIXAR

BRAVE

Merida's Challenge

Adapted by Cynthia Hands
Illustrated by the Disney Storybook Artists

A GOLDEN BOOK • NEW YORK

ISBN: 978-0-7364-2903-0

randomhouse.com/kids

Printed in the United States of America

1098765432

Princess Merida lives in the Scottish Highlands.
She is the best archer in the land.

Merida's best friend is a powerful Clydesdale named Angus.

King Fergus is a strong warrior and Merida's father.

Queen Elinor believes in royal traditions.

The young princes, Harris, Hubert, and Hamish,
are always ready for an adventure!

Circle the picture that is different from the others.

1

2

3

4

5

ANSWER: 4.

As part of her royal training, Merida learns how to tame falcons.

Playing an instrument is a royal tradition—
but Merida does not enjoy her mother's lessons.

Merida learns sword-fighting from King Fergus.

Merida is a skilled archer.
Circle the bow that matches the one Merida is holding.

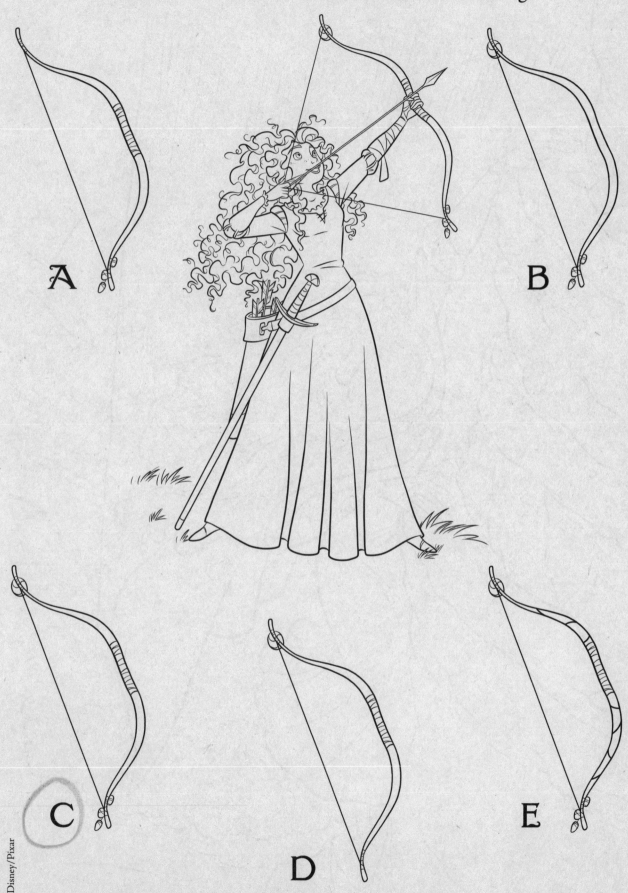

A

B

C

D

E

In her free time, Merida climbs a high cliff called the Crone's Tooth.

Merida would much rather spend the day
with Angus than study royal traditions.

Queen Elinor and King Fergus are very different,
but they rule the kingdom well together.

The royal family lives in a very big place.
Place a mirror on the dotted line to find out the name of their home.

Castle DunBroch

King Fergus takes good care of his hunting dogs.

Elinor tells Merida that she must follow tradition and marry a young man from one of the Highland clans.

Merida does not want to get married!

Fergus helps Elinor with the plan to find a husband for Merida.

How many times can you find the word ANGUS in the puzzle?
Look up, down, forward, and backward.

G A U S A
A N G U S
N G S G N
S U G N A
A S U A S

The longships arrive with the Highlanders from nearby lands.

Elinor helps Merida get ready to meet the lords and their sons.

Wearing a fancy dress is a tradition Merida does not like.

Elinor explains the rules of the Highland Games. The firstborn of the great leaders will compete for Merida's hand in marriage.

Reluctantly, Merida chooses archery as the
contest to win her hand in marriage.

© Disney/Pixar

Bagpipes are played when the lords enter the castle.

Lord MacGuffin and his son are very protective of their clan.
Draw a line between each picture and its two close-ups.

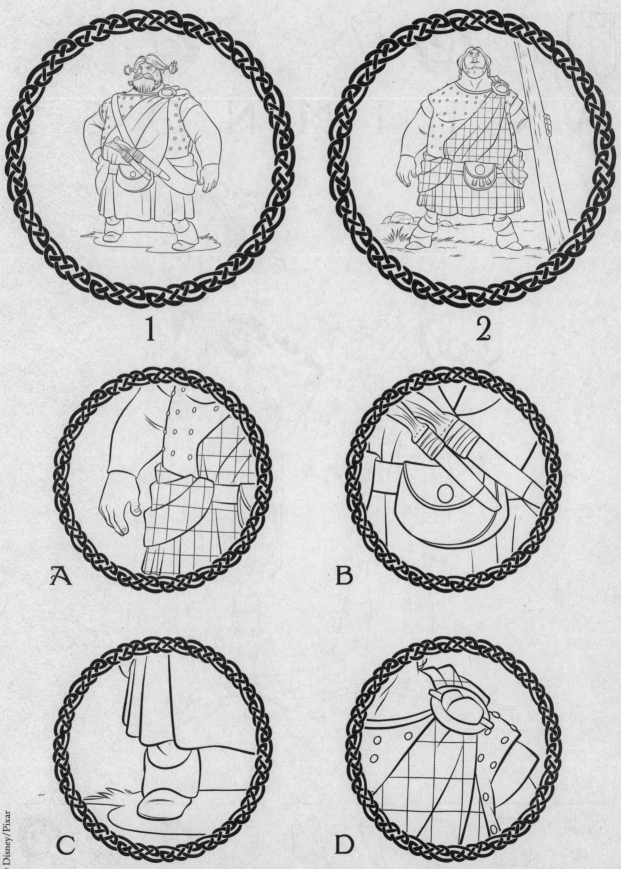

1

2

A

B

C

D

ANSWER: 1-B and 1-C; 2-A and 2-D.

The Highlanders who wear war paint believe their clan is the best.
Use the special code to find out the name of their clan.

A C H I M N O S T

Lord Dingwall and his son are always up for a challenge!
Circle the two pictures that match exactly.

1

2

3

4

5

6

ANSWER: 1 and 5.

The Highland Games are about to begin at Castle DunBroch.

Harris, Hubert, and Hamish are always looking for sweets to eat.
How many muffins can you count?

The archery contest is open to the firstborn of the Highland lords.

Wee Dingwall shoots an arrow and hits the bull's-eye!
Look for five things that are missing in the bottom picture.

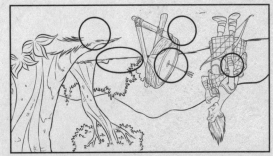

ANSWER:

Fergus looks for Merida, but she is gone!

Merida looks mysterious. Is she going to compete in the contest, too?

No one can beat Merida when it comes to archery.

Merida tells Queen Elinor that she does not want to marry.

Merida angrily destroys the family tapestry with her sword.

Merida leaves the castle and rides Angus into the forest.

Merida falls off Angus near a place called the Ring of Stones.

Merida meets the small forest sprites.
To learn what they are called, replace each letter
with the one that comes before it in the alphabet.

_ _ _ _ ' _ _ _ _ _ _ _ _ _

XJMM P'UIF XJTQT

ANSWER: Will o' the wisps.

Merida finds a witch's cottage in the overgrown Highland woods.

The Witch is very old, and her cottage is even older.
Circle the five items that are hidden in the picture.

ANSWER:

The Witch agrees to help Merida.

The Witch creates a magic potion in her cauldron.

The Witch makes a cake. Anyone who
tastes it will be under a magic spell.

Merida returns to Castle DunBroch with the
spell cake and looks for her mother.

Help Merida find the path to Elinor.

START

1

2

3

FINISH

Elinor takes the cake from Merida, and soon the spell is cast.

While Elinor is away, Fergus entertains
the Highlanders with stories and songs.

The lords want to know who will marry Merida.

After eating a bite of cake, Elinor turns into a bear!

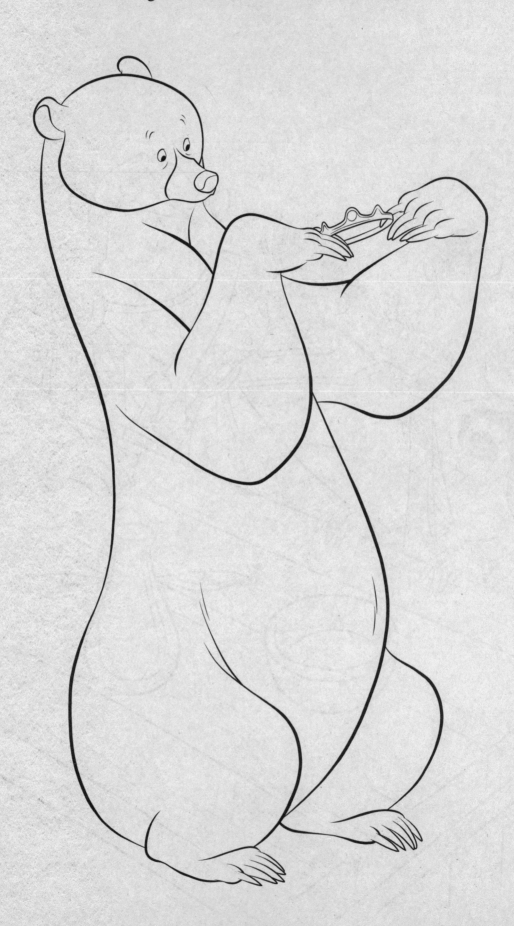

The queen tries to walk, but it's not easy.

Fergus smells a bear in the castle and tries to find it.

The queen must hide from Fergus.
Help her find the way to Merida.

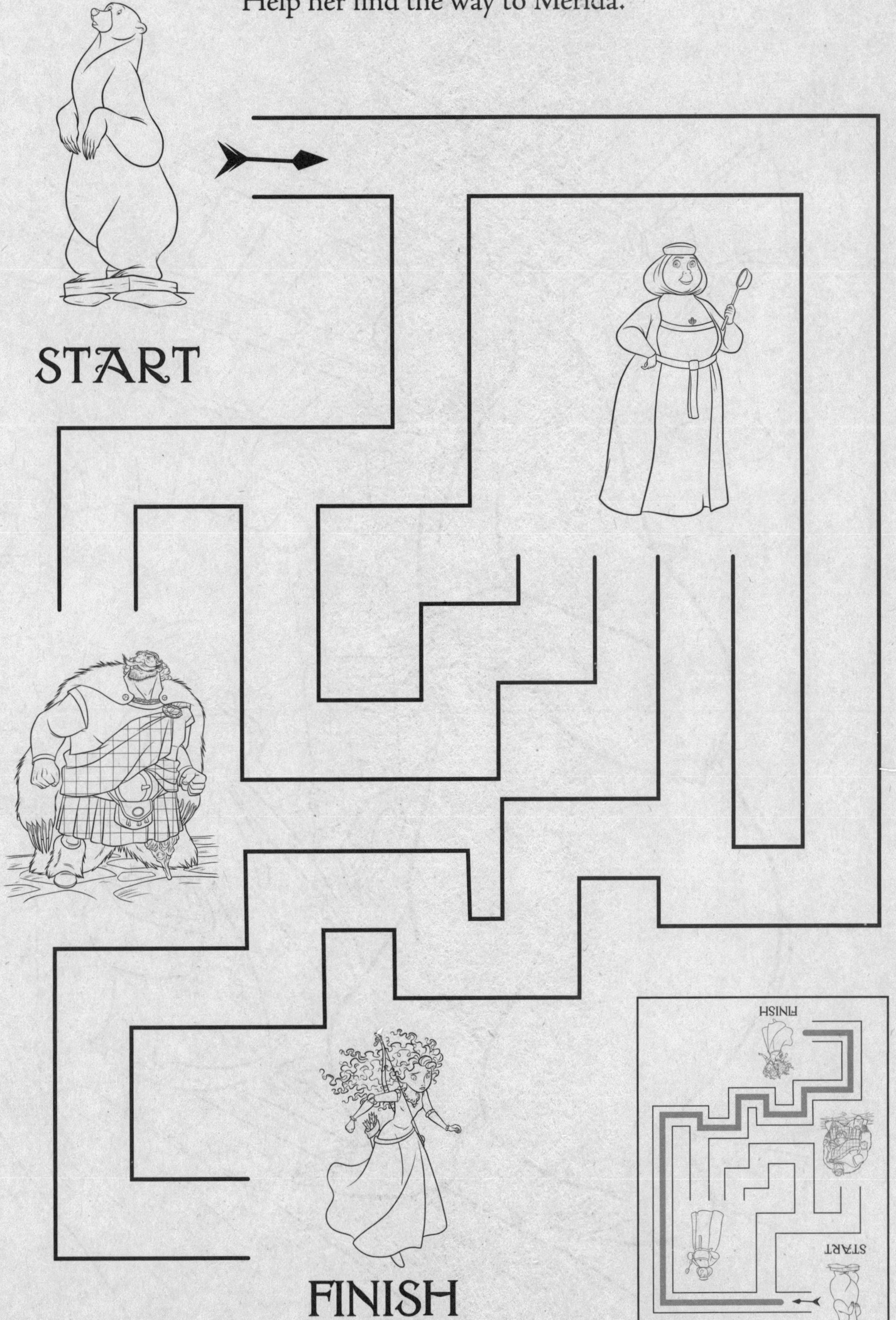

START

FINISH

Maudie, the triplets' nursemaid, is very
surprised to see a bear in the castle.

Harris, Hubert, and Hamish are not afraid of the bear.
They know it is their mother.

The triplets love sweets! Nothing can stop
them from eating the Witch's cake.

Find your way through the maze by spelling the word CAKE
three times. Begin at the arrow and go sideways, up, or down.

➤ C K K E C
A A A E A
K E C C K
C K E K E

Merida and the queen go back to the Highland
woods to look for the Witch's cottage.

From the top of the castle, Fergus looks for the bear he smelled.

The young lords use their strength to open the door of the castle.

Connect the dots to see what is making Young MacGuffin laugh.

Merida wants to find a way to break the spell,
but the Witch and her cottage are gone!

Merida's mother digs through the ruins of the cottage,
hoping to find something to make her human again.

After spending the night in the cottage
ruins, the queen makes breakfast.

Merida gives her mother a few lessons about being a bear.

The queen learns how to catch fish in the river.

How many fish can you count?

ANSWER: 7.

The will o' the wisps return to show Merida
and the queen a new path into the forest.

The wisps lead Merida and her mother
to the ruins of an ancient castle.

The castle ruins look dangerous, but Merida is brave.

Merida looks at the stone tablets and realizes that
Mor'du is the selfish prince from an old legend.

A long time ago, Mor'du was a man, but the
Witch's spell turned him into a bear.

Circle the picture that is different from the others.

1

2

3

4

5

ANSWER: 3.

Merida bravely stands up to Mor'du and protects her mother.

The queen and Merida work together to escape from Mor'du.

On the way home, Merida realizes how she can break the Witch's spell.

Help Merida and her mother get back to Castle DunBroch.

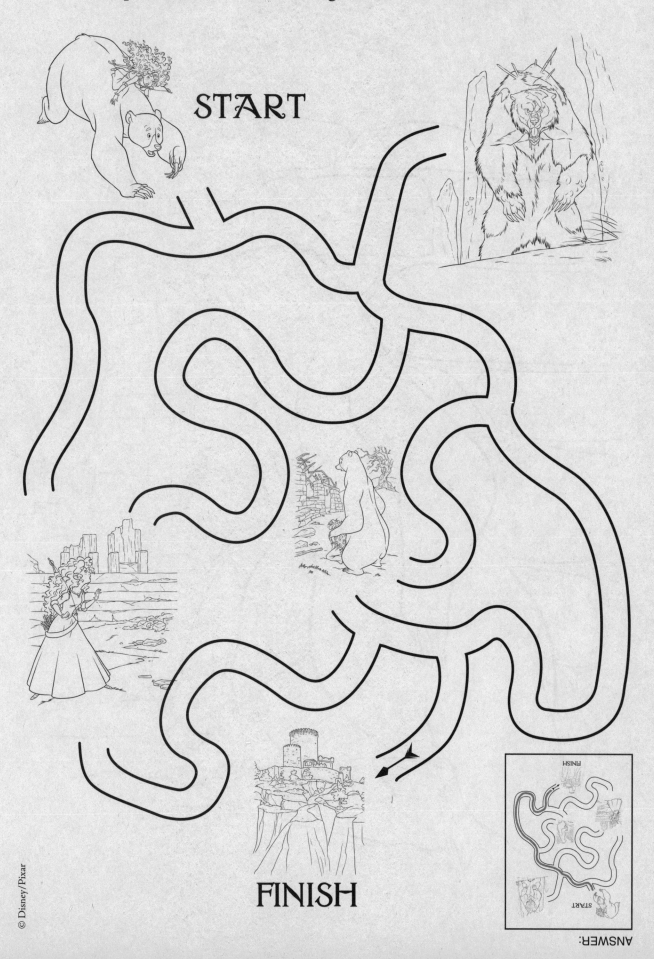

START

FINISH

ANSWER:

Merida and the queen hide from the castle guards.

Merida promises to break the spell and save her mother.

The door to the Tapestry Room is locked, and Merida needs the key.

Trying to hide, Elinor pretends to be a stuffed bear.

Harris, Hubert, and Hamish eat the
spell cake and turn into bear cubs!

Follow the lines to find out the names of the identical bear cubs.

HARRIS HUBERT HAMISH

The bear cubs want to help Merida, so they run
to get the key to the Tapestry Room.

Merida must repair the tapestry to break the Witch's spell.

Merida protects Elinor from her father,
who does not know that his wife is a bear.

Circle the three close-ups that match the
different parts of Fergus in this picture.

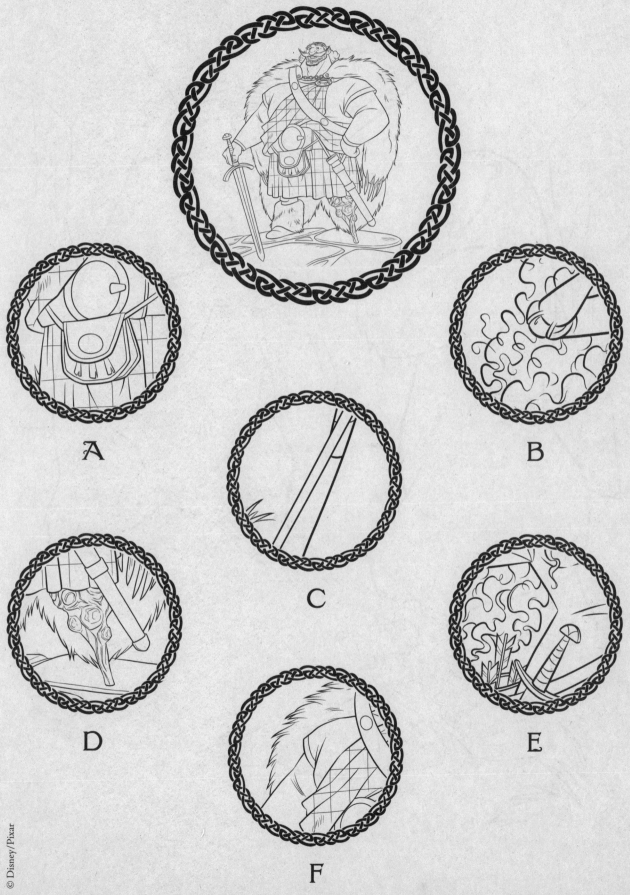

A

B

C

D

E

F

ANSWER: A, D, and F.

Elinor bravely fights Mor'du—and defeats him!

Merida tells her mother that she loves her—even if she is a bear.

The Witch's spell is broken, and Queen Elinor is back.

King Fergus is glad when the three princes are little boys once again.

Cross out all the *K*s and *Q*s. Then look up, down,
forward, backward, and diagonally to find all these names.

MERIDA

ELINOR

FERGUS

S C O T L A N D
R O N I L E Q U
Q H T K Q M K N
K Q A R E K A B
S U G R E F N R
Q K I Q R B G O
K D Q K Q I U C
A K H A M I S H

HARRIS

ANGUS

Look for more words:
DUNBROCH and SCOTLAND

HUBERT

HAMISH

ANSWER:

S C O T L A N D
R O N I L E Q U
Q H T K Q M K N
K Q A R E K A B
S U G R E F N R
Q K I Q R B G O
K D Q K Q I U C
A K H A M I S H

Merida and Queen Elinor work together to make a new tapestry.

Queen Elinor is happy to start new traditions
with her daughter, the brave princess of DunBroch.